Bartholomew Quill

A Crow's Quest to Know Who's Who

Thor Hanson • *Illustrated by* Dana Arnim

little bigfoot
an imprint of sasquatch books
seattle, wa

To Noah, from Papa —Thor

*To Bill, for your unstinting faith,
support, and love; and to Tegan,
with gratitude —Dana*

Manufactured in China by C&C Offset
Printing Co. Ltd. Shenzhen, Guangdong
Province, in November 2015

Published by Little Bigfoot,
an imprint of Sasquatch Books
20 19 18 17 16   9 8 7 6 5 4 3 2 1

Editors: Tegan Tigani and Christy Cox
Production editor: Em Gale
Design: Anna Goldstein

Library of Congress Cataloging-in-
Publication Data is available.

ISBN: 978-1-63217-046-0

Sasquatch Books
1904 Third Avenue, Suite 710
Seattle, WA 98101
(206) 467-4300
www.sasquatchbooks.com
custserv@sasquatchbooks.com

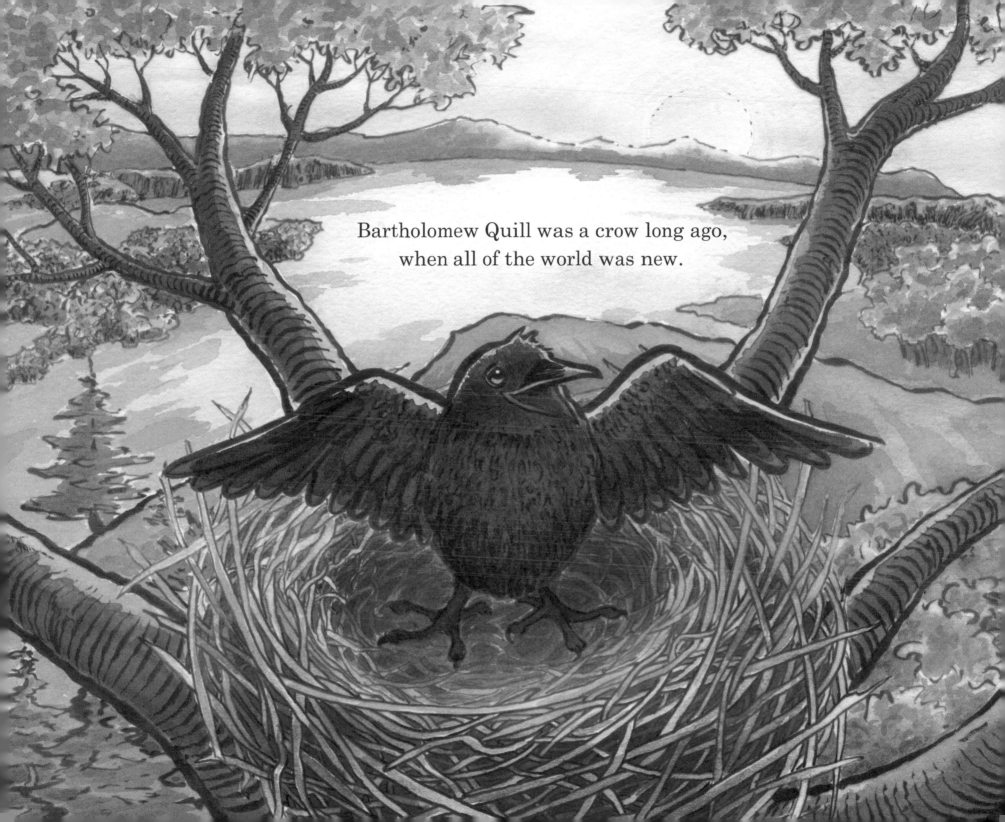

Bartholomew Quill was a crow long ago,
when all of the world was new.

When the bears and the bees
and the hares and the trees
were learning to tell which was who.

Bartholomew flapped and Bartholomew flew
on wings that were feathered, not fuzz.
He could see he was black
from the front to the back,
but he still did not know what he was.

So he soared to the edge of the ocean
and called to a bird on a wave,
"Am I one of you?
Do I do what you do?"
And this is the answer she gave:

"I dive and I float
     in a waterproof coat."

"My diet is fish and crustacean."

"We're both black and sleek,
but you lack a bright beak,
so you cannot be my close relation!"

Bartholomew bowed to the puffin
and found a large bird in a tree,
to whom he addressed
the following test:
"Could it possibly be you're like me?"

"I spend my days soaring and hunting.
Sharp eyes are my favorite feature."

"It's clear that your tail
and your head are not pale,
so we can't be the same kind of creature."

Bartholomew thanked the bald eagle.
Then he searched from the sky to the ground,
in forests, on peaks,
down rivers, up creeks,
but no one like him could be found.

The wolves and the moose were too hairy,

the seals and the salmon too wet.

The heron too tall,

the sparrow too small.

The beetles and slugs smaller yet.

At last he encountered another
with feathers as black as the night.
"Could we be the same?
Please tell me your name!"
This time he had to be right!

But the bird only croaked and flew higher
and turned on its back in the air.
"Related to you?
But I'm larger times two!
My name you can guess if you dare."

"A raven?" Bartholomew wondered,
"The bird best known for its guile?
Well, if he looks like me,
then my looks must be
like the bird with a similar style!"

So he flew to a natural mirror,
a lake that reflected the sky.

And when he looked in,
looking back was his twin,
with the look of a rook in his eye.

"That's me!" Bartholomew shouted,
"The cleverest thing with a beak!"

"And now that I know
I must be a crow,
I'll announce it whenever I speak!"

Bartholomew Quill was a crow long ago,
And a crow he remains to this day.
If ever you doubt it,
just ask him to shout it—
"Caw!" is the thing that he'll say.

GET MORE OUT OF THIS BOOK

Group Discussion

Before reading the story, ask readers to study the cover of the book and use *who*, *what*, *where*, *when*, *why*, and *how* to ask questions such as:

• Who do you think the story will be about?

• What do you think you already know about crows?

While reading the story, ask readers to identify and discuss the rhyming words.

Discuss with students why the raven might be "the bird best known for its guile." Discuss the question, "Do animals plot and scheme?"

Have readers retell the story answering the question, "What is the central message of Bartholomew Quill's story?"

Group Activities

Create a framework poster to gather evidence from the text that demonstrates readers' understanding of the differences among the animals in the story. After the introduction of each new animal in the story, fill in the blank poster together by asking readers:

• What is the animal?

• What are its features?

• What are the functions of its features?

Have readers compare ravens and crows, conducting shared research for a writing project.

Independent Activities

Ask readers to compare and contrast the puffin and Bartholomew by creating a chart.

Ask readers to write a report on an animal of choice from the story, describing all of its features, such as the structure of its beak and how it uses it. Use digital tools to produce and publish the writing.

TEACHER'S GUIDE

The above discussion questions and activities are from our teacher's guide, which is aligned with the Common Core State Standards for English Language Arts that can be adapted to Grades K–5. For the complete guide and a list of the exact standards it aligns with, visit our website: SasquatchBooks.com.